Trash Twisters

WeWrite Kids Book #53

Written by
WeWrite Kids

Carlos A., Tyler A. D., Lizbeth A. A., Stephanie A.,
Luella B., Marco C-H., Brian E.Y., Said G-A.,
Angel G., Greta G., Mariana H., Jose H.,
Cole L., Mariano L.C., Xhunaxhi L.G., Kimberly M.G.,
Jose M.C., Omar O.F., Owen P., Natalie R.,
Alex R-N., Claire R., Isai R.M., Kyla S.,
Joshua S., Aiden T., Nicolas V., Analysia Y.

Illustrated by
Joe Barcelone

WeWrite LLC
Ben Lomond, California

WeWrite
BOOKS BY KIDS - FOR KIDS!

For information regarding WeWrite Kids Books or
WeWrite Book-Writing Workshops and products,
contact:

WeWrite LLC
11040 Alba Road
Ben Lomond, CA 95005
831•336•3382
800•295•9037
fax 831•336•3382 (call first)
www.wewrite.net

Project Coordination and Writer:	Delores Palmer, WeWrite President/CEO
Location and Background Coordination:	Dan Haifley, Executive Director;
	Laura Barnes, Education Coordinator;
	O'Neill Sea Odyssey, www.oneillseaodyssey.org
Coordination, Facilitation, and Writer:	Jody Lust
Illustrations:	Joe Barcelone
Editing and Proofreading:	Jan Hansen
Book Layout:	Bill Kersey, www.kerseygraphics.com
	Alex Bentley, www.bentleywebsites.com
Book Cover Illustration:	Joe Barcelone
Book Cover Design:	Bill Kersey, www.kerseygraphics.com
Photography, Videography, and Research:	Gail Kinstler, www.businessvideocreations.com
Photography & Website:	Alex Bentley, www.bentleywebsites.com
Workshop Assistance:	Catherine Phipps, Taylor McCrady
Printer:	Community Printers, Inc., www.comprinters.com

Trash Twisters
ISBN 978-1-57635-104-8 softcover
WeWrite Kids Book #53

Reducing The Ocean's Plastic Soup

The delightful story you're about to read was developed by Jody Lust's fifth grade class at Gault Elementary School in Santa Cruz, California, during the 2013-2014 school year. Ms. Lust's class had participated in O'Neill Sea Odyssey before they started working with the WeWrite team on this book.

Thanks to Ms. Lust's patience, hard work and willingness to redefine a teacher's educational boundaries to work with O'Neill Sea Odyssey and WeWrite Books on the development of *Trash Twisters*, you'll be able to enjoy a story firmly rooted in a real-life problem: the plastic soup that can be found in parts of the world's vast, dynamic ocean.

O'Neill Sea Odyssey, started in 1996 by surfer and wetsuit innovator Jack O'Neill and his son, sailor Tim O'Neill, engages fourth to sixth grade youth with hands-on science field trips aboard a 65-foot catamaran on Monterey Bay, and in a shore-side education center, in addition to ocean science curriculum provided for use in the classroom. It is free, and each class completes a community service project. The program achieves educational standards using ocean concepts, while teaching youth about watersheds that flow to the sea and their responsibility to protect them. A study of the program's long-term impact found that 75 percent of students who participated in OSO five to seven years before had retained knowledge about non-point source pollution, as well as the stewardship needed to prevent it, taught in the program's ecology curriculum.

That stewardship is needed now more than ever. The ocean covers about 72 percent of the earth's surface. It's the world's largest habitat, its water and vast currents create weather and influence our atmosphere, and phytoplankton at the bottom of its food web produce half our planet's oxygen produced from plant life. It also absorbs excess carbon from the atmosphere. It's also under stress from a variety of causes, one of those being the millions of tons of human-made garbage and pollution—including plastic—that enters it each year. Eighty percent of it comes from land.

The non-profit Algalita Foundation has produced research that found in the North Pacific Gyre, an area bounded by a complex network of ocean currents, "plankton abundance was approximately five times higher than that of plastic, but the mass of plastic was six times that of plankton." This problem was brought to public attention by Capt. Charles Moore, who accidentally encountered a region of mostly plastic floating waste in the Pacific Gyre sailing from Hawaii to Long Beach in 1997.

Sun, wind and saltwater photo-degrade plastic into smaller pieces that retain its polymer structure. The pieces can't be seen from a distance and most are below the surface, suspended in the ocean's water column. There is debris at the surface, though it's only intermittently visual.

A couple of years ago my friend and respected gyre researcher Anna Cummins told me, "Whether you cross the North Pacific, North Atlantic, Indian Ocean or South Atlantic—we just returned from the latter—and drag a trawl on the ocean's surface for one half hour to an hour, you will very likely find plastic particles. Not many, up to a teaspoon, but you find them consistently. Across the South Atlantic, we dropped our trawl every 60 miles across 4,000 miles of ocean, and found plastic in every single sample."

Much of the pollution that finds its way to sea could have been prevented from getting there. Re-using products that otherwise are thrown away is one way to do this, reducing the amount of soil and fertilizers washed downstream is another, and helping other people to do that same thing is yet another. This is part of what O'Neill Sea Odyssey does: educating youth about ocean pollution and providing them the tools to be advocates for ocean health.

Trash Twisters is a fun-to-read story with a very real purpose. Its authors, the students of Jody Lust's class, have written a fascinating story based on the real-life problem of ocean pollution. Enjoy!

Dan Haifley
Executive Director
O'Neill Sea Odyssey

O'Neill Sea Odyssey catamaran

Foreword

Despite increased recycling and compost efforts in recent years, garbage pollution is still a major issue in our planet's future health. Alongside global warming, garbage pollution and littering remain some of the biggest preventable threats to animal wildlife and the environment that the world has ever seen.

Using the power of numbers, the next generation is letting their voice be heard on this pressing issue through an engaging and entertaining book that gives a glimpse into the mind of a child. The talented group of kids behind this book aim to raise awareness of the dangers of garbage pollution through their Garbage Monster character, and prove that any voice can make a difference—no matter how small.

As a previous WeWrite kid author, I can attest to the power of that message, not only in all of WeWrite's books, but in the future lives of the authors. Giving a child a pen and letting them know that what they have to say matters is an empowering piece of the authoring process, especially in a world often filled with "no." Though not all will continue on a literary path, the lessons instilled of group work, collaboration, and being open to the ideas of others will make a lasting impression on the authors' future endeavors.

I am one of the few in my group who continued on in life to become a writer, and for those young readers who dream of one day doing the same, I have three pieces of advice: never give up, write a lot, and trust yourself. Nothing worth having in life is easily obtained, so work hard and put your heart and soul into everything you write—and do it often because practice makes perfect. Lastly, always take the time to listen to the advice of others, but in the end trust your instincts because it'll be your name on it.

Melissa Lewelling
Co-Author of *A Goo Idea!*
(a WeWrite Book)

Table of Contents

Chapter 1 - Mr. Awesomeness

Nicole and Jayden were ordinary kids who did ordinary things like walking the dogs and brushing their teeth. Worries like grades and pimples were normal. They had ordinary friends...well, most of the time. All in all, they had a pretty ordinary life, but things were about to change.

"I can't believe we really did it! What are the chances?" asked Nicole. "We must be dreaming," replied Jayden. "I've never won anything before in my life!" "You're only ten," replied Nicole. "Seriously, Jayden, I've never won anything either and I'm two years older."

Just a few minutes earlier, the siblings had heard of a contest on their favorite radio station. "This is George Frank and you're listening to 106 FM. Today, one lucky family will receive an all-expense paid adventure to a tropical island paradise. This could be you. Keep that dial tuned to 106 FM and if you're caller 106, you'll win the trip of a lifetime," the DJ announced. "Let's go to line 8 right after this song. Stay tuned."

Nicole convinced Jayden to call, just for fun. "We're probably not going to win anyway. I already asked Mom and she said we could try."

Jayden grabbed the phone and dialed. Busy signal.

"Try again," Nicole insisted several times.

It rang, then again, then once more. Finally, a familiar voice answered. "This is 106 FM. You are our 106th caller.

Do you know what that means?" It was George Frank, Mr. Awesomeness.

Jayden almost dropped the phone. "I won?" he questioned.

"That's correct," the voice replied. "You're the lucky winner of the trip to an island paradise!"

The song on the radio ended and Jayden heard the voice on the phone say, "Listeners, you can stop calling. We have our winner!"

Still shaking, Jayden and Nicole ran toward their mom and wrapped their arms around her. "We won! We won! We'll even get to go scuba diving!"

"Are you serious?" Mom asked. "Wait until we tell your dad. We'll finally get to use our scuba diving certifications."

The kids bounced around, on top of the world. They sang constantly for the next month and told everyone who would listen about their prize.

Finally, trip day came.

"Is everyone ready?" Dad asked.

Dad beamed at both children as they drove to the airport. "I still can't believe you two won this trip. We surely couldn't have gone on such an adventure otherwise."

When they arrived at the airport, it was very noisy. Everyone was going this way and that.

Nicole looked up at the board and found Flight 4321, then pointed. "It's Gate 14."

"Great, all the way on the other side of the airport," Jayden complained. "My bag is so heavy. Can we please get one of those carts?"

Nicole asked, "What did you put in there?"

"Stuff..." Jayden replied slyly.

"You brought it, you carry it," Nicole said, annoyed.

Arriving at the gate, they heard, "Flight 4321 now boarding at Gate 14."

"That's us. Just in time," called out Jayden,

"Everyone stay together," Dad reminded them.

As they boarded, the flight attendant greeted them with a friendly, "Aloha."

Mom sighed, as she sank into the cushy chair, "First class, wow!"

"Can we get some peanuts?" Jayden immediately asked. When Mom shook her head "no," he busied himself exploring around his seat.

After a few minutes, there was a sudden rumble. Jayden shouted in fascination, "I think they ignited the engines!"

"Yippee kii yi yaaay," added Nicole, as the plane lifted off. "We're flying!" Jayden squealed with a big smile.

Mom and Dad just grinned at their kids. They were happy to be on their way to a wonderful and unexpected vacation. "Who would have thought...?" Mom whispered to Dad.

As the plane rose higher, Nicole thought to herself, "The cars and buildings seem so tiny from up here. Are those even cars? They look like ants."

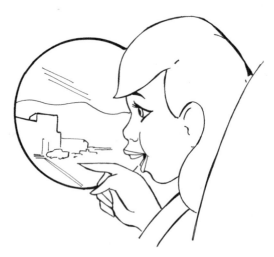

The jet engines droned on and on, making her drowsy. Hours later, all Nicole could see was ocean. "I can't believe how big it is," she exclaimed.

Jayden, always interested in his stomach, munched on peanuts. "These are some good-diggity-bomb things."

Nicole noticed Jayden had his headset on. "Typical Jayden," she thought, turning her attention back to her book, absorbed in the story. Meals, snacks, a movie, and her book helped pass the time.

Chapter 2 - Tropical Tour

"Palm trees, I see palm trees," Nicole blurted out as the plane approached the island. Jayden scrunched in next to her to look. "Jayden, don't push!"

Soon they exited the plane and walked through the airport, collecting as many "Welcome" leis as they could. Jayden waved and called to everyone, "Aloha." Dad motioned them over to the waiting tour bus. Smiling, the tour guide looked down at the two kids. "And what are your names?"

Nicole immediately blurted, "I'm not allowed to talk to strangers."

Mom stepped in, explaining, "It's OK this time, we're with you. This is Jayden and this is Nicole."

"Nice to meet you. Sit wherever you like and buckle up. The 'Welcome' tour is about to begin."

As the bus moved along, amazing sights appeared on both sides. "This is just like a stereo nature show," Nicole laughed as her head swiveled right and left.

They saw a cool rainbow between two volcanoes and dolphins jumping in the ocean. Jayden shouted, "Look, there are seven dolphins. No, wait. There are seventeen," trying to count them as they jumped.

Dad used American Sign Language to Jayden and Nicole to say "no" when the kids jumped out of their seats, too excited to sit still.

Through open windows they could see the palm trees waving among the small thatched houses, with coconuts lodged in the long, spiky leaves.

Just when Jayden was thinking about something cool to drink and wondering what coconut milk would taste like, the tour guide announced, "Well, folks. Welcome to WitchyWitchy Falls. Short walking tours are available for those who would like to explore the cascade trails. We'll see you back on the bus at 1400 hours, that's 2:00 pm. Don't be late."

"Yaaaay" erupted Nicole and Jayden at the same time. They were ready to explore the island. Mom stepped in, "Let's have lunch first, then explore."

Jayden ran ahead, hungry as always. "Yes. Lunch, then explore."

Chapter 3 - Under the Sea

The next morning, over breakfast in the lush hotel courtyard, Jayden and Nicole slurped juice served in pineapples. The family planned the day. Mom wanted to go shopping. Nicole wanted to go horseback riding along the volcano trails. Jayden didn't want to do either of those. "Dad, you promised we could go scuba diving. After all, we won a free scuba adventure and I really want to swim with the dolphins we saw yesterday," he whined. "Sure, why not?" agreed Dad. "Yaaaay," bubbled Jayden through his straw.

After breakfast, the family arrived at the dive center. They were greeted by the dive guide who checked their certifications and gave each of them a wetsuit, mask, snorkel, and fins. They all quickly started getting into their wetsuits.

Wiggling and hopping, Nicole laughed at the acrobatics they were going through to get their wetsuits zipped.

Meanwhile, the guide loaded their regulators, buoyancy compensators, weight belts, and tanks onto the boat, and hollered, "All aboard!"

Weight Belt, Flippers, Mask, Regulator, Buoyancy Compensator, and Tank

Jayden squealed with enthusiasm. They sped off toward the dive site with spray flying from both sides of the boat. The guide gave a briefing about the volcanic reef they would be seeing underwater. He then checked their tanks to be sure the air was on. One by one, they put on their buoyancy compensators (BCs), masks and fins, and sat on the gunnel with their feet planted on the boat deck. The dive guide instructed them to put their regulators in their mouths and roll backwards into the water on the count of three. Jayden, of course, made the biggest splash.

Slowly they drifted downward toward the reef.

Their guide was watching to make sure everyone stayed close together as they became familiar with the new gear and surroundings.

Swimming deeper and deeper, everyone pointed out the brightly colored fish, eels, starfish and coral. It was exciting to explore this new world of the sea. The teal water was silky and cool on the little bit of skin showing on their faces.

Suddenly, Nicole saw a flash of light out of the corner of her eye. She looked right and watched as a colorful butterfly fish with a big spot swam into the coral to hide. The water was so clear she could even see the overlapping scales and tiny geometric patterns of each fin.

The dive guide signaled to Jayden and Nicole's parents to come look. He had found a beautiful nudibranch on the wall. Both parents were entranced by the animal's beauty.

In the meantime, Jayden discovered a cave that he couldn't resist. Nicole gestured for him to come out, looking over her shoulder for the guide. Jayden waved wildly for Nicole to follow him, as he continued on. Nicole knew they should stay with the group, but how could she let her little brother go alone? She reluctantly followed.

Before they knew it, they were chasing a turtle and a school of small fish through the cave. "This is magical," Nicole thought to herself, concern floating away with the bubbles.

Jayden swam down and pointed at a couple of baby white tip reef sharks. Bubbles drifted past Jayden's mask. He could see that the rock was volcanic and striped, with dark purple veins. It looked rough and ancient, almost as if it had been there for billions of years!

The cave was actually more of a tunnel that twisted and turned as it went deeper. Jayden kept swimming, followed closely by Nicole who now had no choice but to keep up with him. Determined to find the end of the cave, he kept swimming. Beams of light poked holes through the dark water. There was just enough light to make out what was around them.

Suddenly, the tiny fish scattered in all directions. Something big and dark swam up from behind them.

Jayden was afraid, wondering if it was a shark. He grabbed Nicole and pulled her into a small indentation in the side of the tunnel. Fear pricked down his spine. His eyes opened wide. When they looked down, they noticed the water was a different color and a bit blurry. It also felt warmer. "This must be a thermocline," Jayden thought.

Wanting to get away from whatever was behind them, they continued swimming toward the larger opening. Jayden saw it and thought, "This looks like where we came in. Good!" The kids swam up to the shimmering surface of the water, expecting to see Mom and Dad.

Sure that her parents were waiting, Nicole ran the whole story through her head. Explaining about following the turtle into a cave, she could blame Jayden for all of it when Mom and Dad asked where they went. They broke the surface and both kids scanned the water for Mom and Dad. No Mom. No Dad. No boat.

Little did they know, at that very moment back on the dive boat, Nicole and Jayden's parents were beside themselves. Mom was sobbing, "How could they be lost?"

The guide radioed the Coast Guard. He relayed the boat's location and reported the children missing.

Chapter 4 - Stranded

Treading water, Nicole saw that the beach was close. She motioned Jayden to head toward it. "Mom and Dad must be back on shore," Nicole thought.

As they kicked on the surface, a wave shoved them towards the beach. They rode the surf as it lifted them up and carried them along. When they got close, they took off their fins and walked ashore.

Finally on solid ground, they took out their regulators and pulled off their masks. Both Jayden and Nicole were breathing hard and sat down on the sand to catch their breath. "I don't see Mom or Dad," Jayden said nervously.

"They should be right here," Nicole replied, looking up and down the beach.

"Where is everyone?" Jayden asked.

Both took off their scuba tanks and pulled off their wetsuits, sinking their toes into the soft black sand. They looked at each other and shivered with a kind of glee. "Swimming with the turtle was really fun, wasn't it?" Jayden exclaimed.

"Yeah," replied Nicole, uneasily. "But let's go find Mom and Dad! I bet they are on the other side of this hill." They sprinted up the oddly-shaped hill. It was beautiful, tropical and warm. Palm trees swaying in the breeze dotted the shore. "Whooaa," Jayden exclaimed as he saw the sun reflecting off the sand, making it look like the sand was moving.

When they got to the top of the hill, nothing was familiar. As far as they could see, they only saw a higher hill. They looked at each other, disappointment in their eyes. Neither wanted to, but they had to admit they didn't know where they were. Nicole murmured, "We might be lost."

Jayden didn't say a word for a while. Then, "Remember Dad always says when you are lost, it's best to stay where you are, as long as you are safe."

Nicole nodded in agreement. Her eyes focused on something. "I think I see a waterfall over there. It must come out somewhere." Then she looked up. The sun was low in the sky and she moaned, "Uhh, it's going to get dark soon."

"We should make some sort of shelter," Jayden offered bravely, as the sun dipped low on the horizon.

"Look, there is some driftwood down the beach," Nicole replied, her voice sounding brighter than she felt.

"It will be just like camping in our yard, when we make a tent with branches and a blanket."

"Yeah, like camping in the yard," agreed Jayden, feeling a little better. He ran off to get to the driftwood first. Nicole began to follow too, but stopped and scanned the beach again for Mom or Dad. She saw no one and buried her worry behind a brave face.

Jayden called out, "So, where do we build it?"

"Over there," Nicole said, pointing.

He nodded and started dragging pieces of the driftwood to the spot. After many trips, they began to create a makeshift shelter. It looked a little like what they built in their own backyard.

They laid big leaves on the ground and put their wetsuits on top. Jayden sat down, bouncing a little, like testing a mattress. "We did it," Jayden announced, with a thumbs up. Nicole nodded as she sat down next to him, quietly.

She stuffed their wetsuit hoods with leaves and put them on their beds. Patting them like Mom always patted their pillows, "There, we have our beds." Tugging the sleeve of her rash-guard, she continued. "Boy, am I glad we had these under our wetsuits. Kind of like your 'pjs.'"

They looked around and realized it was really getting dark. Feeling all alone, both kids scooted closer to each other. Neither said anything as they listened to the waves on the beach.

Jayden started to miss his parents. A lot. His sister had told him their parents would find them, but he wasn't so sure. He was getting hungry. "Where is Mom? Where is Dad? I'm hungry. And thirsty."

Nicole, trying to be brave, reassured him, "They'll find us in the morning. Don't worry."

They were hungry, tired, thirsty, and scared. Nicole and Jayden clung to each other, rocking and exhausted. Waves lullabied them to sleep, with both sinking slowly into their beds.

Chapter 5 - Exploring

The sun was shining when Nicole woke up. The sound of waves rushed in, filling her head loudly. Without moving, she could see Jayden was still sleeping, curled up next to her. Beyond him, she could see the beach and ocean through the driftwood. "Oh, I remember now," she whispered to herself.

Jayden stirred, stretching his arms above his head. Nicole always loved the way he woke himself up, even when he was little. When his hands pushed against the driftwood side of the shelter, it moved. "Uh oh," she thought.

"Jayden, don't!" she whispered loudly. "Huh?" he asked, sleepily. "What's wrong? Where...?" As he looked around, he remembered too.

Then his face puckered up, beginning to cry. "Where's Mommy? Daddy?" Nicole hugged him closer, trying to think of what to say. He hadn't called them "Mommy and Daddy" since he was five, when he heard from his friend that was what babies said.

A few minutes later his sniffling slowed down and, wiping his eyes with his sleeve, he said, "I'm hungry, Nicole. I really am."

"I'm hungry too. And thirsty. But we need to go to the top of that mountain so we can see where the boat is anchored. I'm sure everyone is looking for us."

Jayden began to pout, but then stood up, straightening his shoulders. "Let's see if we can find where that waterfall comes out." Nicole looked at him proudly and smiled a bit.

Setting out in the cool morning, they climbed toward the hill where they were yesterday, but went another way, watching for signs of water. They came to a small but thick wall of vegetation. Nicole walked up to it and started kicking away the brush and vines. A big green snake watched them from the branch of a vine-covered tree as she worked.

"C'mon Jay, we have to make a hole if we want to get to the other side. We have to get to that mountain," Nicole whined, urging him to help. Jayden sighed and joined in the kicking. After what seemed like hours of pushing through the thick wall, they made a hole big enough to fit through. Sticks poked them and made their feet sore.

At last the tangled vines gave way and Nicole yelled, "Jayden, look!" Her face beamed and her whole body seemed to light up in the sun.

"Nikki, it's a stream, and it's not too far from camp!" Jayden exclaimed. But Nicole didn't answer. The moment she saw the water, she ran up, stopped to look at it to make sure it was deep enough, then ran back a few feet and flew into the air, making a cannonball into the water. "Woohoo!" she yelled, worries evaporating for the moment.

Jayden laughed and cannonballed in after her, trying to make a bigger splash. They swam and drank happily for a while, until Nicole said they should get to that mountain.

Hesitantly, they continued on, following the stream until they found the thundering waterfall they had seen the day before. Climbing to the top, around the volcanic rocks, they discovered the waterfall led to a little lake. They kept going up until they got to the top of the mountain, scratched and scraped. Jayden was the first to arrive. Holding the walking stick he found, he held it high in the air. "I made it!" he gloated to Nicole, who was still climbing, struggling behind him.

When she got up to where Jayden was, they stood side by side, their bodies turning together in a 360 degree circle, searching for something familiar. No hotels. No boats. No people. No Mom. No Dad.

"Oh no. It's an island. Not the mainland. Maybe it's an atoll," breathed Nicole. "We're lost. How are we going to get off?" They both started crying, sinking slowly to the ground with exhaustion and despair, not quite believing what they were seeing. Jayden muttered quietly, "How could we be lost? We'll never get home."

Through her tears, Nicole blubbered, "We'll find a way." Jayden was looking at something down at the edge of the water, his face wet with tears. "What's that stuff? Looks like a dump. Is it trash?" All kinds of trash piled in an endless heap was strewn across the beach as far as they could see. Jayden just whistled a low, "Whewwww, what a huge mess."

Nicole looked down to where he was pointing. All she saw was trash. She squinted and shielded her eyes from the sun. "It's high noon. We need to get back to our camp. Maybe Mom and Dad are there. Let's follow the stream back. At least we know it comes out near our camp."

Backtracking, they followed the stream around the hill. Jayden kept thinking about the trash. "If there's trash, there must be people."

Interrupting his thoughts, Nicole pointed. "There it is. See? Our camp is right over there." Disappointed, Nicole sighed. There was no one there. "Let's look for food. Remember those palm trees that are everywhere? I'll bet we can find some coconuts."

"Okay," said Jayden, his face brightening. He loved coconut meat. It snapped and squeaked in his mouth when he bit a piece off from a bigger chunk. Dad had let him use the hammer to crack a coconut shell at home. Jayden smiled, remembering how the shell and coconut meat smashed and went everywhere when he hit it too hard. That was cool!

With his feet squeaking the sand as he scuffled in little steps, Jayden set off to search for fallen coconuts. He was happy with this new important job, finding food.

Nicole looked around the island. She saw something move in a bush near the edge of the water. She watched for a moment, then slowly went over to look.

Among the exposed roots of a nearby palm tree were oysters, all laid out on a rock. Twelve oysters, arranged neatly in two rows. They looked ready to eat!

"Somebody did this, but who?" Wondering out loud, she looked around quickly. No one. She looked around again. Nicole's stomach grumbled. "So hungry." Sniffing the oysters, she remembered that their family ate them at home and these seemed fine. She picked some leaves nearby, glancing around. Then she folded them around the oysters and headed back to the shelter, calling to Jayden.

With three coconuts in his arms, Jayden crowed. "Nicole, look what I found!" "Sweet!" she called back. They both reached the shelter saying at the same time, "Man, I'm so hungry!" "Jinx." "Double jinx."

Jayden looked at the big smile on Nicole's face and then at what she was carrying. As she unfolded the leaves, his eyes opened wide. "How did you get those?" he questioned, dropping the coconuts in surprise.

Nicole explained, "I saw a bush move and found them on the rock over there. But no one was around." Both kids eyed the oysters hungrily. Jayden reached for one but stopped right before he bit the meat, looking at Nicole. She sniffed them again. "They seem perfectly OK," she said, not quite sure of it herself. Hesitantly, Jayden took a bite. "Mmmm, not bad. I could live with this. Tastes just like the oysters at home." As they ate them, they started to debate about how the oysters got there.

"I say it was aliens," guessed Jayden. "Be serious!" said Nicole. "Oh, OK. It was a unicorn then," Jayden replied. "I think it was a person," Nicole said. "So you're saying there is another person here?" Jayden asked. "Or there was," Nicole said. They both shivered at the thought. Then she added, "You have a better idea?"

"I'm really thirsty," Jayden whined. "We need something to carry water in," Nicole said, looking at the coconuts. "For now we can drink coconut milk."

"Right," said Jayden and began singing, "I've got a lovely bunch of coconuts. Look at them, all standing in a row." Nicole smiled and said, "Let's go look for a rock to open them." "OK," Jayden replied. Both kids ran out of the shelter, racing to be the first to find a good rock. Jayden ran back to the shelter with two rocks, one with a pointed end, perfect for cracking coconuts.

Jayden started banging on the coconuts. It was hard. "Whew!" Jayden said, wiping his forehead. He pounded harder, cracking one, but the coconut milk started to pour out onto the sand. Nicole quickly picked up the coconut, letting the milk drip into her mouth. Jayden grabbed at it, saying, "Hey, me too!" But it was gone. "Don't pound so hard on the next one," Nicole said.

As he hit the next coconut, trying to make a hole, they both sang as Nicole danced and jumped around. Jayden got a hole poked in both coconuts, careful to not hit too hard. With a proud smile, he handed Nicole one. "Yes!"

They drank coconut milk until their bellies were sloshing. It was the second time since arriving they felt carefree, if only for the moment.

Finally, Nicole and Jayden giggled, fell on their backs and sighed. "We should probably look for some more food tomorrow. Fish or something." Jayden nodded, then said, "Yaaay, sushi."

Listening to the waves for a few minutes, as the twilight sky turned from orange-red to cobalt blue, they settled into their shelter. Jayden quietly asked, tears running down his face,"I wonder where Mom and Dad are?" Nicole sighed, putting her arm around him. "We'll stay right here, like Dad said, so they can find us. Maybe they'll find us by morning. Let's cross our fingers. Tomorrow, we need to think about food, water and how we'll survive."

The waves covered the silence, both thinking their own thoughts. In a quavering voice, Jayden piped in. "We can go look for a good stick and make a spear. For sushi." "Tomorrow Jayden, tomorrow." Above the sounds of the waves floated a low moan, an eerie sound. Sleepily, Jayden whispered, "What's that?" Nicole answered, "Just the ocean," pushing her fear away. "Count the rhythm of the waves. One...two...three...," she trailed off, and Jayden made a soft, "Zzzzzzzz."

Chapter 6 - Survival

Jayden was up early, at the crack of dawn, searching for just the right stick.

He loved sticks and making a spear to catch fish sounded fun. "I'm still hungry," he thought, finding a branch about three feet long and a shark tooth, partially buried in the sand. He ran back to Nicole and she showed him how to tie the tooth to the spear with some plastic she found.

"Perfect!" Jayden exclaimed after re-tying it several times. Proud of himself, he handed it to Nicole for approval. "Nice! Maybe it's even lucky," Nicole beamed. He immediately ran to the ocean.

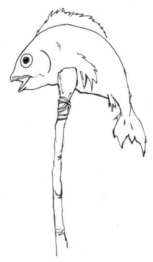

After many failed attempts, Jayden thought to himself, "I'm not giving up!" He zeroed in on a fish and let his spear fly through the tide pool. "Yahooooo!" he yelled, holding his wriggling prize high in the air. "We're having fish tonight!"

Grinning from ear to ear, Jayden was pleased with himself, as he scouted for more prey. "Dad said that determination always pays off." He also remembered another "Dad" lesson: "Practice makes perfect." Thinking of his dad made catching the fish even sweeter.

Nicole kept an eye on him as she scouted the area for more food. A shiny light caught her eye. It was a broken bottle. Terrific. They could use that to start a fire, like Dad showed them when they were camping.

With her piece of broken bottle, Nicole headed to the beach to show Jayden. On the way, she saw some crabs trying to scurry away. Yes! She broke off one of the big leaves that grew everywhere and grabbed the crabs, wrapping them in some leaves she folded up like a bag. Nicole felt wonderful. Powerful.

Inside the leaf, the crabs tickled her hand as they tried to find ways to get loose. Just then, she heard Jayden yell again about his fish. Nicole ran to him, holding her prize high in the air as she repeated, "Yahooo!"

Heading back to camp, they chattered about their prizes. Jayden was excited about the piece of glass. He loved trying to burn things in the sun at home. Nicole always felt sorry for the ants and bugs that crossed his "SunRay." Grabbing a piece of coconut to chew on, he set out to find some small pieces of wood and dried things for a fire. Jayden sang out as he ran, his mouth full of coconut, "Mmmmm, I can just smell the barbecued fish. We're going to eat like kings tonight."

Back at the shelter, Nicole wondered to herself, "What was that creepy sound we heard last night? What could have made it?" Fear shook through her, but she forced herself to focus upon what they needed to survive.

"Now we have water, food, and shelter. We will survive. But for how long?" She tried to hide her fears from her brother's eyes. He was so excited. He was having fun. For now, she told herself firmly, "We are OK. We can even use the coconut shells to carry water back to camp."

Nicole realized she would have to kill the crabs with a rock. Ugh! But she knew she had to do it. She felt sorry for them as she hit them.

Wrapping the dead crabs in leaves, Nicole headed to the stream with two coconut shells to get her mind off the crabs. Glancing at Jayden as he searched for dry fire-starters, she filled up the coconuts.

It didn't take long for him to gather materials. Jayden dumped his armload outside the shelter while Nicole carefully scrunched the coconuts into the sand so they wouldn't spill. "There, now we have a water supply."

Jayden began shredding dried wood and plants as Nicole gathered rocks for the fire pit. It was just like camping at home, but this time they didn't fight. Jayden carefully placed his "fire kit" of small dead branches, dried grasses, and dried coconut shell puff in the middle of the rock circle. Using the broken glass, he started focusing the sun on the fluffy starter material. He held the glass still. Nicole watched as he worked, amazed that he could stay so still. That wasn't like Jayden.

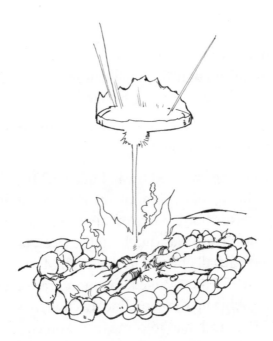

It seemed like a long time until they saw a wisp of smoke. Jayden blew gently on it, trying to coax the smoke into a flame.

"I hope this works," Jayden muttered, as he aimed the piece of glass at the twigs. First it smoked, then burst into a tiny flame. The fire was lit. "Hah. I told you it would work!" Jayden exclaimed.

"I never doubted you," Nicole replied. They added brush to the sparks until a small fire warmed the rock they would use to cook the fish and crabs. "Now we have to gather more brush and sticks so we have a supply."

Feeding the fire, Jayden began singing again, at the top of his lungs, "We're going to eat like kings tonight." He picked up a forked stick from his pile and handed it to Nicole, proudly. "Here's a fork for cooking."

"Great," she smiled. She felt good, too.

The fish and crabs cooked on the hot rock tasted wonderful. Through a mouthful of fish, Nicole mumbled "Mmmmmm. Good." Jayden just kept stuffing his face.

"After we eat, there's still time to walk along the shore." Jayden nodded in agreement.

As they walked, they noticed trash. Lots of it. They had seen it from the top of the mountain. There were shredded plastic bags, plastic bottles, lots of flip flops, and even bottle caps and straws. Trash was caught in the trees, tangled in the roots, and partially buried in the sand. Most of it was plastic. The further they walked, the more trash there was. It appeared to gobble up the shoreline. Each wave seemed to add more. "This trash had to come from someone. Maybe we can find them and they can get us off this island," Jayden said, repeating what he said on the mountain.

Nicole just nodded. She had an idea about the flip flops piled everywhere. Loading her arms up with flip flops, she thought, "Why not make something out of them? Like sleeping mats. I could weave them together with plastic strips or…."

Interrupting her thoughts, Jayden ran off to grab the end of a rope sticking out of the sand. "Help me, Nicole. It might be something we can use."

"Well, I already have things we can use. Look. These will be for sleeping and sitting on. I'll make sit-upons."

"Nicole, come help me pull this," Jayden whined. "Oh, OK," she muttered, dropping her idea and load for the moment.

Together they pulled on the rope. "Look," she said, "I think it's a boat fender. Remember, like on the dive boat? It seems stuck. Pull harder." As they were pulling, they heard "Aroooooooo." It was a deep, dark, howling sound echoing through the surf. "Aroooooouhhh."

"What is that?" Jayden asked. "I don't know, but I do know we don't want to find out. Let's get out of here," Nicole replied.

"But I want that fender," Jayden pleaded and kept pulling. He yanked on the rope again. "Aroooooo," the low, howling sound rumbled again, kind of like a fog horn under water. Jayden worriedly said, "That sounds really scary. This time you're right, Nicole. Let's get out of here."

He dropped the rope and they both sprinted all the way back to camp.

Breathless and scared, they huddled by the fire in silence until the first bright star appeared in the sky. "Let's make a wish," Nicole whispered, noticing Jayden's gaze at the same star.

They watched the fire dancing in the breeze until it died down. Nicole yawned and gently guided Jayden, who was nodding, inside the shelter with, "Let's go to sleep." Jayden started to protest. "I'm not...."

"Sleep!" Nicole cut him off. "Go to sleep. Tomorrow, we fish some more. And build a better shelter." He relaxed, closed his eyes and almost immediately began dreaming of his success at spearfishing.

Jayden was fast asleep when Nicole heard that creepy sound again, only this time it sounded almost sad, or lonely. It was like it came from the belly of some terrible thing or place.

Chapter 7 - Flip Flop Mattress

The next morning, Jayden stretched, pushing against the side of the shelter, then opened his eyes with a jolt. He'd been having a dream where he and his sister were stranded on a deserted island. It had been interesting but he was glad it was just a dream. Turning his head, he saw waving palm fronds. "Wait a second," he thought. Looking around he raised himself on one elbow. It hadn't been a dream. He was still here! And there was Nicole, still asleep.

He looked around again and remembered the nightmarish sound. Nicole woke up too, and looked at Jayden's worried face, knowing what worried him. "It's OK, Jayden. We'll be fine. We'll go fishing again today. And build a shelter that won't move when you touch it. And we can explore some more." Jayden's worry disappeared. He loved being "Chief Explorer" and always wanted to be out in front.

Thinking about the boat fender and what he might be able to use it for, he decided they should go back to that trash pile and get it. Later.

Nibbling some fish left wrapped in a leaf, they felt a little better. The tropical sun, hot already, climbed through the morning sky.

Nicole asked, "What do you want to do first?" "Let's go get stuff for our house. Then we can fish when we're hot," he suggested.

"Good idea," Nicole agreed.

"Let's go over to that big pile of driftwood and see what we can find," Nicole suggested. With a "yeah, race you there," Jayden sprinted off. Nicole just let him win. He had cried enough for one vacation.

Jayden climbed up on top of the pile, waving a stick and yelling, "Champeen! I won!" just like he did at home. Nicole felt a wave of homesickness wash over her. But she smiled bravely and raced up next to him, waving her own stick.

From the top, they looked around. Strips of plastic, bottles, broken objects, flip flops and Styrofoam were all tangled together with the driftwood. Jayden looked disgusted. "What a gnarly mess!"

After poking around for a while, they began carrying sticks, logs and a few old soggy boards back to their camp. When Nicole asked Jayden to help carry a heavy piece, he even did it without complaining.

"Look at this piece," Jayden whistled. "It has teeth marks. Big teeth marks."

"Oh, be quiet," responded Nicole uneasily, remembering the large dark shape underwater. She also wondered again, "Who brought the oysters two days ago? What made that eerie noise?" Nicole looked around. She still had that feeling someone was watching them, but saw no one.

"So, where do we build our new palace?" Jayden interrupted Nicole's thoughts, bringing her back to what they were doing. They looked around and decided it should go right where they were standing. Jayden stuck the boards in the sand and went off looking for palm fronds. Nicole found some more rocks and put them next to the shelter.

Jayden lumbered back with an arm full of palm fronds. "Just like we see in the movies." He laid them on top of the shelter, then picked up the rocks and put them on top of the palm fronds. The roof collapsed.

"Jay!" shouted Nicole. "What?" asked Jayden. "You messed it up!" "Me?" shouted Jayden. "What did I do?"

"You messed it up."

"If you want to think that, fine!" and he stormed off.

"I can't believe he just left," Nicole muttered. "What a baby. Does he think this is easy for me? I hope he'll be OK. But when I get hold of him, I'll...."

"You'll do what?" Jayden said. Nicole almost jumped out of her skin. "Quit talking to yourself and let's build this hut."

Before Nicole could respond, Jayden set to work. She watched in awe. It was like he was instantly older. First he dug four holes in the sand. Then he put the corner poles in, one by one, packing wet sand and big rocks around each pole, just like he did with Dad when they went camping. Finally, the crooked branches stood up almost straight. Out of the corner of his eye, Jayden spotted what looked like a tattered piece of plastic sticking out of the sand, way down the beach. As he pulled it, a long, ragged remnant of black plastic came out.

"Oh!" He thought to himself, "I'll use this to make a rope so I can tie palm fronds to the poles." When he was done, he had a flat, low roof almost like a lean-to. Bowing low at the waist and with a wave of his hand, Jayden beckoned Nicole into his palace with a beaming smile.

"Wow, look at the great hut you built," Nicole admitted, marveling at what he had done. "I'll go get some more leaves and palm fronds for the floor and roof. This will work just fine," she said approvingly. "And flip flop mattresses and sit-upons would be a perfect touch, too," her thoughts returning to the pile of flip flops.

Jayden tried to hide his smirk. He felt proud of himself. He felt grown-up. "Just wait until Dad hears what I did." Grabbing his spear, Jayden marched off toward the beach. "I'm off to get more food," he announced triumphantly to Nicole, who was still fixing the roof. Jayden did seem more grown-up, Nicole thought to herself. But she only said, "That's good!" out loud.

When Nicole was satisfied with the roof, she headed over to where Jayden was fishing, hoping to find more crabs or something they could eat. "Oh good, more crabs," she said, capturing ten crawling ones and adding them to her leaf bag.

Jayden was also getting better at fishing and held up his spear with a wiggling fish. "Yaaaay! I'm going to try for another one."

Nicole nodded and turned back to camp. She could see Jayden was fine in the clear, shallow water. She also wanted to start the fire this time, before he came back to argue that it was "his" job.

Jayden arrived back at camp, happy and laughing about his two fish just as Nicole got a good fire started. She caught the look of surprise on Jayden's face but turned away, trying to hide her smile.

With the meal over, the two looked at each other, more relaxed than they'd been in days. Except for their bug bites, homesickness and sunburns, they felt pretty good. As they listened to the waves, darkness came in, and gentle breezes rustled the palm leaves.

"Our hut looks pretty good. And we have enough food left over for breakfast," Nicole murmured sleepily. "We can go exploring tomorrow. Yeah, tomorrow we'll see what's around."

"And get that fender," Jayden nodded in sleepy agreement. Sleep pushed away the uneasy feeling that someone was still watching them.

Chapter 8 - Big Surprise

Morning came with the gentle sound of waves in Nicole's ears and Jayden's usual stretch, along with his yawning "Unngghhh." But this time, the shelter didn't move dangerously. "We did good," Nicole thought as she looked around. Things weren't quite so scary. Food was still folded under a leaf in the corner of their hut next to the "coco-teens," as Jayden called them. "Maybe Mom and Dad will come today. We're staying put, just like Dad told us."

Jayden sat up, looking at the ocean. "Hey, it's low tide. Let's go explore the tide pools. Maybe we can find some mussels or trapped fish there."

"Good idea," Nicole agreed as she reached for the food packet and handed Jayden a coconut canteen. "We need to get more coconuts too."

Jayden piped in, "I want to climb coconut trees. Some of them grow low and sideways, kind of parallel to the ground. I can reach them and you can catch."

"Well, let's go down to the rocks and tide pools first. See what we can find," Nicole suggested. Jayden grabbed his prize spear and they set off toward the rocky shore.

As they worked their way around the bend, Jayden saw something move below on a crag. He motioned to Nicole to come. Whatever it was, it was stuck in the garbage and seaweed. As they got closer, Nicole exclaimed, "Whoa!"

"What?" Jayden shouted. He stopped in his tracks.

They saw a large fish tangled in a fishing net. It was struggling to get free but the more it wiggled, the tighter the net wrapped. As the fish flopped over, Jayden looked closer. He could see a girl's head and shoulders and a body covered in green scales. She looked at him with desperation in her eyes. Nicole and Jayden just stood there, frozen.

"Please, help me get out," she whimpered weakly. "I've been here for a long time and now I'm easy prey! The fish are nibbling my fingers. My scales are drying. I'm surely going to die." She began to cry. "Please help. Help me." Just then a large wave rolled up, battering her. As the water rolled back to the sea, the fish-girl coughed and choked. "Please help me. Please. I'm begging you."

Jayden sprang toward her first. "It talks! It's a girl!"

Cautiously, Nicole tried to size up the situation, saying, "Whatever she is, she is so weak, she's probably not much of a threat to us." Jayden announced, "We have to find something to cut the net now!" He spun around toward the fish-girl. "Hold on. Hold on. We'll get you out."

"Jayden!" Nicole barked. "Go that way. I'll go this way. See if you can find anything sharp. Now, go!" They split up. Nicole ran back to the hut to get the piece of broken glass.

Jayden found a broken abalone shell and then a rusty Swiss Army Knife in a tangle of garbage. He also found a cracked plastic bucket, perfect for carrying stuff. "Jackpot!"

Nicole ran back with the piece of glass, holding it up to Jayden. "This'll do."

"Okay, but beat this!" He was fumbling with something. "I finally got it open." The sun glinted off the Swiss Army Knife he was sharpening with a rock.

Running back to the fish-girl, Nicole yelled, "We found a knife! And I have a piece of glass."

"Hurry," she whimpered weakly. They went to work.

"Thank goodness," whispered the fish-girl. "Cut me out, fast! The great white sharks are probably circling. They know I'm weak."

"Okay," Nicole replied, looking around for dorsal fins. The kids continued to saw away on the tough, old net. They looked closer at the fish-girl, who had now stopped moving. But she was still breathing, her eyes closed. "Are you a mermaid?" Jayden asked softly.

She replied weakly, "Yes. Hurry. Do you see any sharks?"

Nicole turned and scanned the ocean. "No, not right now."

Finally, they cut through enough of the net so she could wiggle out and squirm back into the water.

The waves closing around her, she turned and looked back at the two kids, their mouths open, still in shock.

"Thank you!" The mermaid slowly swam away, leaving only the tangled net among the garbage and seaweed.

With his eyes glued to where she disappeared, Jayden asked, "Was that a dream?"

"If it was, it was a pretty wild dream!" Nicole replied shakily. "This is really a strange place!"

As they stood there, Nicole questioned, "I wonder if she's the one...."

"Who left us the oysters?" finished Jayden.

"I don't know," Nicole replied with a shrug. Jayden put his knife in his pocket and began jumping from rock to rock, ready to do something else. "Let's explore some more," he said.

Nicole wasn't ready to move, shaking her head about what they had seen. "Let's start on that," pointing to the wad of net still floating among the rocks. "We might be able to use it."

"OK," agreed Jayden, who loved searching for treasure. He was still thinking of the fender as they pulled out the net. "Shish-kabobs!" Jayden hollered, spearing the fish still tangled in the web. Triumphantly, he tossed the catch into his new fish bucket.

"I'm really thirsty," Jayden complained, hanging his tongue out of his mouth like a puppy. His lips were cracked and swollen on his sunburned face.

Nicole didn't answer, lost in thought, still thinking about the mesmerizing mermaid and that eerie sound in the night.

On the walk back to the hut, she wondered if their parents would ever find them.

At the hut, they grabbed the coco-teens, trying to quench their thirst. Jayden noticed how quiet Nicole was and, in true Jayden style, began teasing Nicole about her tangled hair and bright red, spotted face. It wasn't long before they were laughing, creating names for each other like Lobster Monster and Spotzilla.

"What a day!" Jayden exclaimed, trying to make his sister feel better. "We found a mermaid, more water, and I got fish-kabobs, and a bucket! Wait till Mom and Dad...." He trailed off, his voice cracking. A tear ran down his face.

Neither said anything, not wanting to give in to their homesickness. Quietly, they prepared the fire and food, the routine becoming familiar.

Watching the flames dance, both were lost in their thoughts until the soothing sound of waves, the smell of smoky barbecued fish, and memories of the day swept over them. Nicole crawled onto her sleeping spot inside the hut, put her wetsuit over her, and plumped up her hood-pillow. Jayden, never wanting to admit that he was tired, crawled in too.

Both kids fell sound asleep immediately. "Arrooooooooo, arrrrhhhhhgggghhh," echoed through the night. But neither sleeping sibling awoke.

Chapter 9 - Trash 101

The next day started out just like the one before, warm and breezy, with the ocean sparkling before them. As they ate and shared their thoughts about yesterday, Nicole suggested they go the opposite way to explore.

"Sure," Jayden replied. Nicole picked up a coco-teen, in case they didn't find water. Jayden grabbed his trusty spear, and patted the knife in his pocket. "Charge!" He raced off, spear in the air just like he saw in the movies.

Huffing and puffing, Jayden reached the top of the nearby hill first. As Nicole climbed up, Jayden was already on his way down the other side, almost to the tide pools. Just beyond him, Nicole saw something big and grey. "Could that be a shark?" she wondered. "Stop! Jayden, Stop! Don't move a muscle."

"But I saw a leg in the water! It's someone."

"Wait! What is it?" Catching up with him, she grabbed his arm. She looked again. It was a shark in the shallow water. Slowly, it swam toward them. She rubbed her eyes. "Legs?"

"I told you!"

"Jayden, d-d-d-don't go any closer to...whatever it is!" Nicole stuttered bravely, looking at the shark thing. It didn't go back underwater. One eye was looking up at them. It seemed like it wanted to come closer.

Nicole pulled her brother back again. He turned to her, "I'm not scared!"

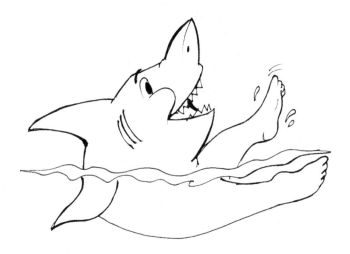

Just then the shark thing opened its mouth and words bubbled out. "Don't be scared. I'm...."

"Aaaahhhhh. It can talk!" The kids yelled in unison, frozen to their spots. Again, it talked in strange, bubbly words. "Don't be afraid. I'm part human, just like you two."

"And part shark," interrupted Nicole.

"I won't hurt you. My name is Shark Boy."

"He seems friendly. I'm Jay...." Nicole flicked his head. "What was that for?" Jayden yelled at Nicole, pushing her hand away.

Looking back at Shark Boy, they noticed he wanted to talk more but was panting. "Do you need to get back into the water?" Jayden asked him, already sensing that he wouldn't hurt them. Shark Boy nodded, easing his body back into the water as the kids moved carefully toward him. They sat down, out of reach, watching him swim through the shallows.

"Did you like the oysters I left you?" Shark Boy asked.

Nicole and Jayden looked at each other in surprise. "We wondered who did that," Jayden said.

Shark Boy continued. "I saw you in the underwater tunnel when you got separated from your parents. I've been watching you. I scared fish up when you were spear-fishing," pointing to Jayden with his fin. "I just want to help...and be friends." With their eyes wide open at what they were hearing and seeing, Jayden and Nicole listened to his strange story and strange, burbling words. "Nothing here seems normal," Nicole thought.

"Why did you swim so far away from your parents?" Shark Boy asked.

Nicole explained, "We were just watching the turtle. Then the fish surrounded us and it was beautiful. We just followed them a little way. They were twisting and turning and then the lantern fish came up to Jayden and he swam away with them. I had to follow to make sure he...." Her voice trailed off.

"Well, that explains it. It is pretty amazing here. Sorry you lost your parents. I didn't see where they went. I thought I should stay with you two, in case you needed my help. It's lonely here. I only have one friend. Most of the sea creatures don't like me. The other sharks are bullies. When they tease me, I go deep underwater to my house, in a sunken pirate ship. I only come out when Sirena comes. She's a mermaid."

"Sirena?" Nicole whispered.

"Yes, she is my only friend. We play underwater frisbee with a shell. Nobody else likes me. But Sirena and I have fun. I even taught her how to talk!"

"We rescued her yesterday. She was caught in a net," Jayden explained.

"Yeah, she told me," gurgled Shark Boy. "She's grateful, but too shy to say so herself."

"We'll be your friends," Jayden replied, with a bold smile.

Nicole announced, "It's high noon, we need to get out of the sun. Besides, I'm hungry." Jayden nodded vigorously, rubbing his stomach. "Come on Jay," Nicole urged, not wanting him to be too friendly.

As they turned toward the hut, Shark Boy called out, "How about some more oysters? I can bring them to you. Just watch for me in the water."

"Awesome," Jayden said. Then, with hardly a splash and a flip of his feet, Shark Boy was gone.

"Cool! He's really cool," said Jayden as he pulled some chunks of coconut out of his pocket, giving one to Nicole. They chewed on the coconut and headed back to camp. It wasn't long before the kids spotted Shark Boy again, splashing the water. In his teeth, he gently carried seven oysters, dropping them on the sand when Jayden ran down to the water's edge. He returned to the water to swim in circles, with only his dorsal fin giving his presence away.

Up at camp, Nicole grabbed the leaf hats and the coco-teens and ran back to the beach.

"Hey Nicole. Oysters! I saved you three." Jayden gloated. "I already gobbled up mine."

Nicole slurped the oysters down. They both watched Shark Boy as he clowned around to entertain them. Jayden and Nicole laughed. "Amazing. No one will ever believe this."

Shark Boy asked, "Have you kids seen the trash beach yet?"

"You mean the humongous pile of junk?"

"Yeah, we call it the Garbage Patch. All that trash floated here."

"But where did it come from?" Jayden questioned.

Shark Boy hesitated, looking back and forth to each of them, trying to figure out if he should tell them the truth. He didn't want to lose his new friends.

"Well," he paused. "The trash comes from land. From humans. Careless humans. Not like you! Humans throw trash on the ground. The litter eventually washes into the storm drains and flows into the rivers which flush into the ocean.

"The trash then gets pushed by the waves and rides the ocean currents. Some of it is caught and eddies up, collecting on the beach. Over time it grows and piles itself up into a knotty mess.

"Plastic doesn't biodegrade. It photo-degrades. This means the sun breaks the plastic into smaller and smaller pieces, kind of like a toxic soup. It can stay for hundreds of years."

Shark Boy continued, "Look at the sand. You can see the bigger pieces. Others are microscopic and are eaten by fish who mistake them for plankton."

"You mean the fish-kabobs have plastic in them? Are those the little things I saw in their guts when we cleaned the fish?" Jayden asked.

"Yes," replied Shark Boy. "It all starts with litter. They just throw it away."

Jayden scooped up the sand. "When you stop and think about it, there isn't any 'away.' It ends up here, and probably other places too."

"That's the big problem," sighed Shark Boy.

Nicole agreed. "Out of sight, out of mind." Then in a stronger voice, she continued, "That's just awful. I'm sure lots of people would care if they knew it existed, if they could see what we see here. We have to get off this island and save the ocean! I'm sure people would care. Without the ocean, no one can survive."

Shark Boy murmured, "Maybe there is hope."

"Wow," Jayden responded, after a long pause, thinking about what he was learning. "But what about the treasure? Is there any? Dad says that one man's junk is another man's treasure. I still want that fender buried in the sand."

"Stop it Jay! We're talking about something bigger."

"Do you know there are at least five places in the world where trash collects?" Shark Boy continued. "They're called 'Gyres.'"

Nicole listened intently, her sharp mind taking notes in her head. "How did you get to be so smart?" "Well, I use to live with a deep water oceanographer. He rescued me after the accident...but that's another story."

Shark Boy's story was broken off when Jayden's attention began to wander as he burst into song. "Gyre, gyre. Rhymes with 'Fire.' Let's go to the trash pile. There might be treasure."

"Ughhh," Nicole groaned. "Trash is collecting everywhere." Shark Boy made a toothy grin. "Ok, I'll meet you back where we met earlier."

Chapter 10 - New From Old

Jayden jumped up, always ready to lead the way. "Look. There are thousands of water bottles. And flip flops."

Nicole grimaced with new understanding, "It's a mountain of useless old trash."

Jayden called back, "No, it isn't useless. Look at this. It's a beach chair."

Nicole argued, "It only has half a leg!"

"We can bury the leg in the sand. Then we'll have a lowrider chair. Perfect for our campfire."

"Fine," she said.

But Jayden didn't hear her. He was already busy grabbing more stuff. He laid his treasure out on the beach in a long line. "This is stuff we need." In his pile was a broken net, rusty flashlight, broken steak knife with barnacles, sunglasses with smashed lenses, a pink and purple boogie board with a broken leash, a large plastic jar with a boat's logo on top filled with slimy stuff, an old shopping cart, a toilet seat, a ripped-in-half flip flop, a frisbee, a doll, a wagon, a table, another fisherman's net, two cups, three jugs, four plastic bottles, bags, and lots of pieces of wood. Jayden hummed to himself, taking stock of his new treasures, his "loot" as he called it.

"You're not dragging all that stuff back to camp," Nicole argued, knowing it was a losing battle. "But then again, this stuff might be useful," she said to herself. Picking out what she wanted to take back first, Nicole began packing things into one of the fisherman's nets. "Ugh, this is heavy. Help me drag it, Jay." Slowly, they hauled it down the beach.

Shark Boy kept popping his head out of the water in different places, having fun with his new friends.

Just then, his expression changed as he thought of something. "Be careful." he warned. "The Garbage Monster thinks the trash belongs to him. You have to sneak it away quietly."

Both Nicole and Jayden dropped what they were holding, frozen in place by what they just heard.

"Whaaa......?" Nicole asked, barely able to breathe.

Jayden said it out loud. "A monster? A Garbage Monster?" Jayden sang out, incredulously.

Nicole asked, "Is that what has been making those scary moaning sounds at night?"

"Yes, I think so," Shark Boy said gently. "He never wants to give up his trash. Every time anyone takes a piece, he moans. It's his soul. He can't exist without it. He thinks the humans are giving it to him to build a plastic island."

Jayden and Nicole were still frozen in place. Then Nicole looked around. "What do we do?"

"Oh, he won't hurt you. At least I don't think he will, unless he catches you taking his trash. He has so much he might not even notice this stuff is gone. Besides, more and more trash arrives twice a day with each high tide."

Jayden broke the spell with, "Don't worry, Nicole. I'll protect you. If he tries anything, I'll jab him with my spear. He'll be shish kabob-ed, just like the fish." Nicole smiled at Jayden's bravado. Then, waving to Shark Boy, agreed to meet him later. Nicole picked up her net, keeping an eye out for the monster.

"Ready Jay?" she called, looking uneasily over her shoulder.

Jayden, his net full of his treasures, bolted forward to be in the lead. It wasn't long before the treasures weighed him down. Trudging along, with the safety of camp in sight, his mood instantly changed. Jayden began to sing quietly to himself, "Happy Birthday to me."

Nicole had forgotten all about his birthday. Jayden had been carving a tally mark each day on the side of the hut.

He was keeping track, knowing that his birthday was coming soon. Had it really been that many days?

Arriving at camp, each grabbed a coconut from the hut. Plopping down on the sand, they drank the cool water, pouring the rest on their faces.

After a short rest, they joined Shark Boy in the ocean, playing tag and body surfing, the foamy waves swelling around them. With the coming of twilight, they sat in the shallow water, sharing their story about winning the vacation.

Shark Boy just listened, his head moving back and forth, enjoying his new friends. When they finally took a breath, he offered, "I have an idea. How about making a raft? Then you can sail to where a boat can see you."

Nicole and Jayden looked at each other, nodding in agreement. "Great! Let's start in the morning. We'll meet at that driftwood pile down the beach," decided Nicole.

"I'll see you then," Shark Boy waved as he swam away.

Back at camp, Jayden sang softly, "Happy Birthday to me."
Nicole gave him a hug. "I'll bet we find Mom and Dad by
your birthday."

Jayden just nodded into her shoulder, letting her hug him.
Then, in usual Jayden style, he spied the piles of treasure and
dug into them. Nicole said softly, "I'll make the fire."

Chapter 11 - Escape Plan

In the morning, they all met at the driftwood pile, loaded with pieces they found the day before: rope, plastic, net and Jayden's knife and spear, which he always carried.

"Hey, I think this big plastic sign will work as a sail," Nicole called, as she pulled out a plastic piece.

Jayden picked up a skinny log, dragging it over to the "Raft Place" with a grunt. "This will be good for the mast, or whatever it's called. It's really heavy, but it looks strong."

Shark Boy observed what they had gathered. "I asked Sirena if she would help too. She'll be here soon. I think we can actually make a raft."

"Sweet," Nicole said. "Look at these things. We can use them like nails. And I found this nice piece of wood. It's beautiful. Like a surfboard, but chewed up a bit."

Jayden said, "Cool. Shark Boy and I found a bunch of rusty nails and a little plastic shovel we can use."

Sirena arrived, dragging some plastic pieces behind her. "Hi everyone."

Nicole and Jayden stopped and waved at her. Nicole called out, "Hey Sirena, thanks for helping." "She really is real," Nicole said softly.

Sirena showed them the plastic things. "I found a whole bunch of plastic bottles to go under the raft, so it will float better."

Quietly, she turned to Shark Boy and asked, "Do you think this raft is actually going to float?"

"Probably not," Shark Boy said softly, so the kids couldn't hear. "Let's not tell them. It will break their hearts. They really just want to go home. We'll keep it between you and me for now. Let them have their imagination." Louder, he said to Sirena, "Look at what we've done so far. Here comes Jayden with another log to attach to the mast."

"Jayden, good for you," Shark Boy said, "That will finish the raft."

Heaving together, they pushed it out into the surf. Excitement was in the air. Jayden shouted, "The raft floats!"

It was almost dark, so they would have to wait until tomorrow to see if the raft would bear their weight.

"Arrrooooaaa." They heard the sound again. This time, it bellowed from the deep. With each angry-sounding moan, it became louder, more frightening. "Arooooooaaaa. Arrooooughhhh."

Jayden started stuttering. "I'm.. I'm... I'm... scared. It's the monster. Let's get out of here."

Nicole took charge. "Let's beach the raft. Everyone push."

Once it was back on the beach, Shark Boy and Sirena hastily said "goodbye" and slipped into the water.

Nicole yelled to Jayden, "Let's go!" Running back to camp, they both frantically squeezed through the hut's opening at the same time, flopping down on their bed, scared and shivering.

Jayden cried, "I just want to go home. Now."

"I know, Jay, me too. Tomorrow we'll launch the raft." She held her brother until his trembling stopped and he was asleep. Then she allowed her tears to flow. Sleep came slowly that night.

Chapter 12 - Wrecked

In the morning, they were quiet; neither one wanted to bring up the monster. Nicole said, "We need to go back to test the raft. Here," handing Jayden some leftover fish. "Let's get going."

On the way to their raft, Nicole said, "If it floats today, we'll load it and leave tomorrow. " But when they got there, they saw it was ruined. "Wha...?" Jayden yelled, as he ran over to it. "It got trashed!" he yelled again. "Smashed into pieces!"

Nicole immediately wondered if Shark Boy and Sirena did it. When Shark Boy arrived he was surprised. He just looked at the splintered pile, stunned.

Jayden was mad. "Who would do this?"

Nicole joined in, "Did you and Sirena do this? You doubted that we could make the raft, I know that. Did you want us to stay here with you so you wouldn't be so alone? We thought you were our friends."

Jayden added, "All we wanted to do was go home."

Shark Boy responded, sadly, looking at what was left of the raft. "We would never do such a thing. We're your friends and want to help you get back home. Look around. Do you see all this trash? It wasn't here yesterday. I bet I know who did this."

Nicole could see floating flip flops, plastic bottles and tangled nets mixed in with pieces of the raft.

She looked around and saw something in the distance. She could only see part of it, a big eye, and what looked like a tail splashing. "Whoaaa! It's humongous! Look!" Nicole pointed. Jayden was speechless. She could tell he saw it too.

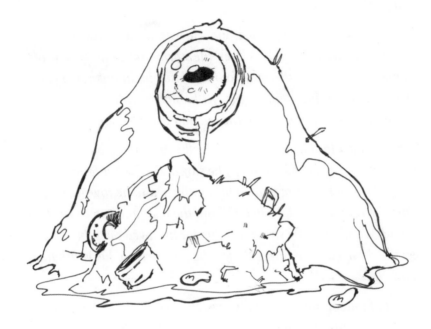

"Is that the monster? The Garbage Patch Monster?" Jayden asked, realizing what they were seeing.

Sirena swam up, having overheard what they were saying. "Yes, it IS big. No one knows just how big or what it really looks like. It seems to morph. It keeps getting bigger, the more garbage it eats."

Jayden and Nicole stood glued to their spot for a long time as they watched.

Nicole asked worriedly, "What is it? Where did it come from?"

Sirena began: "*Once long ago, in ancient times, a fisherman had a newborn son and a wife. He was fishing one day and got caught in a sudden giant storm. The waves became ferocious, no matter how how hard he tried to row his boat home, the storm carried him farther out to sea.*

"*The fisherman held on for dear life. He was at the mercy of the waves and wind. Many days later, the storm broke and gave way to calmer waters. The fisherman found himself in an unknown place. Desperate to see his family again, with only the stars to guide him, he dipped his heavy oars into the sea and travelled for many a day.*

"*Time seemed to slow down, but actually an eon had passed. Finally, one morning as the dawn broke, he saw a distant but familiar shore. Driven by desire to hold his family again, he rowed wildly. Once he reached land, he bolted from the boat and ran toward his home. Wandering the streets looking for his loved ones, bewildered by the changes, he found nothing. The memories of his youth had long since passed.*

"*The unfamiliar and unfriendly new city held no hope for him. Bitterness consumed his soul. He rowed back to the place before time to live out his days, alone and angry. Making a new life in the Garbage Patch, he built a world from his despair and other people's garbage.*

"*You can still hear agony in his moans during the night.*"

Nicole sighed, "How sad," as a tear slipped down her cheek.

Sirena answered, saying, "This is only one legend. There are many. But no one knows for sure." Then she stopped, her eyes frozen on a spot behind the kids. Out of the underbrush appeared a person with a windburned face. "Look!" Sirena said to the kids, her eyes wide with surprise.

Chapter 13 - Birthday Wish

Nicole and Jayden whirled around, as four other people burst into view. Sirena quietly slipped into the water and Shark Boy jumped in with a soft "splunk." They disappeared without another sound.

The leader held up her hand for her team to stop. In surprise, she said, "They're just kids. Are you Jayden and Nicole?"

At the same time, Nicole and Jayden yelled, "Yes! That's us!"

The leader smiled broadly. "I'm in charge of one of the search and rescue teams who've been out looking for you. We're here to take you home."

The air was flooded with tears of relief. Huge smiles appeared all around, reassuring the children that they were safe now. Jayden and Nicole burst out with bits of their story, talking at the same time.

Nicole tried to explain, "We were following the turtle and fish, and got lost...." In mid-sentence, she stopped and looked at Jayden, catching his eye. "Happy Birthday!" she yelled, "Jayden, your birthday wish came true. It came true!"

One man swung Jayden to his shoulders as Jayden yelled louder, tears still streaming down his face, "Yahoo! Happy birthday to me. I'm the champeen. We made it happen!"

All the team members introduced themselves to the kids. The leader said, "I'm Captain Jody of Ocean Search and Rescue. We have someone who wants to wish you happy birthday too." She handed Jayden a walkie talkie and showed him how to push the "talk" button.

"Hello?" Hearing both his parents singing "Happy Birthday," he started crying in relief. "Mommy? Daddy?"

Nicole grabbed the walkie talkie. "Mom! Dad! We want to come home."

The team beamed as they listened and watched, proud to be part of a successful rescue.

After they handed the walkie talkie back, reassured that they would meet their parents soon, Captain Jody explained what had been going on after the children couldn't be found.

"Your parents were in a right fit when they discovered you were missing. We sent out four search parties and have been searching all the islands and atolls in the area. This atoll isn't even on the map. It's really a forsaken place, just a giant dump anyway."

"Thank you, thank you, thank you, for finding us," Nicole said as she hugged Captain Jody. "We were trying to build a raft but…." Nicole didn't finish, not wanting to tell them about Sirena and Shark Boy. She looked at Jayden, changing the subject. "Do you want to see our camp?" Immediately, Jayden sprang off toward camp, spear in hand, yelling, "I'll lead the way. Come on, guys!"

Everyone was impressed with the camp and how well the kids had managed. Jayden gave them a closer look at his lucky spear, Swiss Army Knife, and the piece of bottle they used to start fires. Nicole picked up a coconut, saying, "These are our coco-teens."

Shaking their heads in amazement, the rescuers stood quietly surveying the scene. A collection of broken pieces of trash was set off to the side, ready to be used in new ways.

Chapter 14 - Rendezvous

Breaking the silence, Captain Jody asked, "I just got word. Your parents are heading here in a helicopter right now."

"Wow, yeahhhhh! They're coming here!" Jayden yelled, holding his treasures tightly. Nicole looked around, happy that they'd been found, yet wondering if she'd miss this place. "They'll get to see our camp!"

Jayden immediately began jumping up and down, listening for the helicopter.

While they waited for their parents to arrive, a crew member brought the skiff around the island. Jayden saw Nicole scanning the ocean. She looked fiercely at Jayden and held a finger to her lips; he gave her a knowing nod. Silently, they agreed not to say anything about Sirena and Shark Boy. No one would believe them anyway.

Finally, they heard the helicopter above the waves.

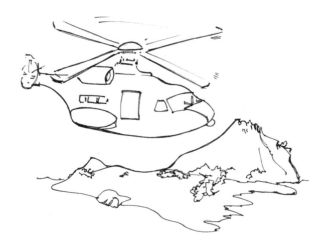

"Here they come! Here they come!" Nicole and Jayden began jumping up and down again, waving their arms like helicopters. Both parents were waving wildly back at them. The helicopter landed, stirring up a cloud of blasting sand. Captain Jody surrounded Jayden and Nicole with her arms, shielding their eyes until the blades stopped and the door opened. She let them run to meet their parents, who leaped out of the helicopter with arms open wide. "Nicole! Jayden!" Dad yelled. "My babies!" Mom blubbered, tears running down her face.

The crew was standing at attention, respecting what they were proudly witnessing: a successful reunion after stress-filled days of tension and searching. Jayden and Nicole looked at their dad, who was saluting the crew. They saluted too.

Both parents could barely contain their emotion. Mom kept hugging them, reassuring herself it was really them. Several times she whispered, "My babies. My babies are safe."

Jayden buried his face first into his mom's shoulder, then his dad's, tears of relief streaming down everyone's faces. No one was embarrassed. Dad told them how proud he was. Jayden was bursting. "We did just what you taught us. We stayed put. And I got a fire going. I stayed really still until it was smoking! And I barbecued fish. Come see our camp."

Nicole, still in a tight hug with her mom, quickly nodded. "Yeah, come see our camp." Jayden held onto his dad's hand as he led the group to their hut.

Nicole let Jayden bombard their parents with how and what they did to survive. Their heads shook in awe and relief as they watched and listened, bursting with pride at how their children had been so clever.

After a while, Jayden ran out of steam. They all just swayed in a group hug, arms wrapped around each other, trying to take it all in. In the middle of the hug, Jayden said wistfully, "That was some family adventure we won."

Nicole nodded, then lifted her chin and whispered, "We really did it, didn't we? But I just want to go home."

The special moment was broken as the crew flew into action. Captain Jody commented, "Oh boy! The press is here already." Dad overheard and asked, "Who's here? Who are they?" "Reporters. They've heard about the rescue over the Coast Guard channel."

Chapter 15 - Live at Five

A news helicopter hovered overhead, looking for a place to land. Three boats appeared around the bend and pulled onto the shore.

Captain Jody ordered her crew to surround the family. They knew what to do as the first reporter and camera crew poured out, trying to scoop the story and make headline news. Everyone jostled for position, trying to be first to ask questions and cover the breaking story. It was chaos as reporters attempted to push through the line of crewmen positioned to safeguard the family. Dad held Jayden close and Mom encircled Nicole with her arm, trying to shield her from the microphones being shoved in her face.

Captain Jody called to the family, "Follow me." She led the family toward the helicopter, telling the reporters sternly that they would have a chance to interview them shortly.

Nicole and Jayden were speechless. Captain Jody looked at their faces, then at their parents. "We will do our best to keep them under control, but they will want to talk with all of you. Are you up to it?" Dad looked at his family, each nodding in agreement. "Well then, we'll set it up for thirty minutes from now, over there at the cove. That will give you guys a chance to catch your breath."

Some of the reporters and cameramen scattered over the area, filming closeups of the camp, and the trash the kids collected, as well as long shots of trash piled along the shore.

The press conference began with an official statement from Captain Jody, describing the events leading up to the rescue. Immediately following, reporters were allowed time to interview the children and their parents. After many questions, Captain Jody announced, "That's all. Let this exhausted family get back to their lives. The press conference is over. Thank you." She led the family away to the helicopter, where they climbed in, buckled up and waved goodbye. A cloud of sand enveloped the reporters as the helicopter took off.

Nicole snuggled into her Dad's arms. Jayden yelled, "Cool! We even get to ride in a helicopter!"

Nicole could see the reporters scrambling over their camp like an army of ants. She was relieved to be rescued but, at the same time, sad to leave the island and her new friends. Nicole reached out and squeezed Jayden's hand. Through her teary eyes, she forced a smile. Jayden scooted closer to his sister. Mom and Dad watched in amazement. The arguing and teasing they remembered were gone, replaced by a bond so strong it seemed nothing would ever break it. The children had grown up and, more importantly, had grown together.

Over the noise of the helicopter, Dad said to the kids, "You know, back in civilization, you are quite famous!" Mom added, "Many people will be relieved that you are safe and sound. Not every story like ours has a happy ending."

"I just want to go home now," Nicole said. "Yeah," Jayden added, "and sleep in my own bed."

As the helicopter turned away from the island, Jayden and Nicole looked back and saw something rise out of the water in the distance.

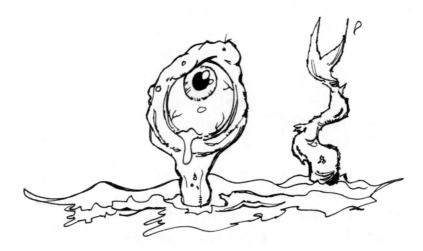

It was the Garbage Patch Monster. Mostly what they could see was one large eye above the surface. It appeared to be sad. As it slipped back into the water, there was a sort of distant moan. Nicole was now sure what it was.

Arriving at the main island, everyone said their goodbyes and Dad thanked the pilot again. A car was waiting to whisk them away to a hotel, far from reporters.

The family hugged a lot that night. Jayden babbled endlessly. Nicole was quiet, caught between what had happened and what was coming.

Chapter 16 - The Mission

In the morning, everyone was subdued on the plane ride home, reflecting on the recent events, and simply worn out. Both Jayden and Nicole were exhausted, but happy.

Back at home, there was a phone call from Walter Crankcase asking Jayden and Nicole to appear on a major talk show to share their experiences on what was now being called "Flip Flop Island."

After some discussion, everyone agreed to have them appear. Many television stations, newspapers, and radio stations, as well as internet reporters, contacted them for interviews. It was fun to be stars and answer questions for a while.

Nicole and Jayden wanted to tell people about the trash, how it was ruining the ocean and harming marine animals.

Something important was happening. Even though they were only children, people were listening to them. The garbage patches were getting bigger all over the world and it seemed like it was their job to tell people about the problem.

Both Jayden and Nicole realized they could still answer questions, tell people how they could clean up the garbage patches, and still keep their secrets.

It wasn't long before even the President of the United States heard about Nicole and Jayden's message. The White House contacted the family, wanting to help. After considering several good options, they all decided on a plan which included an international monument.

The President declared, "FlipFlop Monument will draw attention to the problem and help people learn what they can do in their own neighborhoods to save the ocean and help the animals."

Jayden told his friends about the monument idea. "It's going to be awesome. It will inform people about ocean pollution and how they can get involved. Yeah, it's going to be really cool. It's a pollution solution!"

"Hey guys. Lets write a book about Flip Flop Island."

"Yes! What a great idea!"

Armed with pencils and the belief that kids can change the world, they began to write a little about their own neighborhood. Each agreed that their efforts would multiply with each helping hand.

Grandma always said, "Many hands make light work." So, together, kids can help save the Earth. As they spent mornings writing their story together, Nicole remembered a poster she'd seen by Margaret Mead. "Never doubt that a small group of thoughtful, committed citizens can change the world. Indeed, it is the only thing that ever has."

Nicole smiled. She understood exactly what those words meant. They were doing it. She went back to work with her group, revising their story.

Nicole and Jayden met many people because of their experience. Learning more and more about the ocean and how to take care of it, they became ambassadors for ocean conservation and stewardship. Familiar questions kept popping up everywhere: "So, what's up with this garbage patch and why is it so important? What can I do?"

Jayden and Nicole explained there are at least five of these patches in the oceans, and there are more than just a few pieces of trash floating in the ocean. Some have tiny pieces of plastic that resemble "nurdles." Some have huge pieces. It all gathers together in soupy blobs, maybe even bigger than Texas.

"But it's too big for one person to clean up," Jayden would explain in his best ambassador voice. "You just need to pick up trash in your own town, around your own neighborhood, taking care of your own area. This is your sphere of influence. Don't let the trash get into the waterways. That will help the ocean the most."

Grabbing his lucky spear, always near by, Jayden would raise it high into the air. "Be a champeen. Find your own Spear of Influence. Like mine. The ocean doesn't belong to just one person; it belongs to everybody. We're doomed if we don't take care of it."

Nicole and Jayden thought about how their life had changed, just like Mr. Awesomeness on the radio predicted when they won the adventure. They liked being on his radio station and talking to people. Mr. Awesomeness would announce each time he began one of the interviews with Jayden and Nicole, "I hear that you have been growing your sphere of influence and have been invited to the White House by the President of the United States to share your mission to clean up the ocean. When we sent you on a family vacation to paradise, we never expected it would become a Garbage Patch Odyssey. Remember, it all started here on 106 FM where exciting things happen everyday."

"Stay tuned."

Joe Barcelone
Illustrator

This book project is a great way to satisfy the kid in myself and I love working with kids.

The book has a positive message, and I enjoy being creative with kids and seeing their

Joe Barcelone - Illustrator of *Trash Twisters*
Artist, Cartoonist, Film Director, Screen Writer

imaginations. It's fun to share their excitement and be a celebrity with the kids. Of course, I like to be the center of their motivation.

I've loved watching WeWrite grow and seeing the positive impact of what we do on the kids. I think WeWrite is a unique program that makes kids think and participate at an adult level by using their child's (childlike) imagination.

Trash Twisters offers a creative angle to tackle an important issue using fantasy. And I like drawing monsters. I love watching the authors act out characters and scenarios and how much they are willing to get involved in an idea.

At the beginning of the project, I noticed that the kids were scattered when it came to ideas. Later on they became more cohesive and focused; then it became about working together.

I look forward to working on more WeWrite projects with creative kids and helping them develop their imaginations.

Jody Lust
Facilitator

Before this project, my class wrote because they had to. Afterwards, they wrote because they had something to say. By doing the research, they gained a knowledge and understanding they could draw from when developing the characters and story.

Photo by Alex Bentley

Jody Lust
Master Teacher, Writing Coach

These writers truly believe this book will make a difference. This book starts a dialog about what can be done to save the turtles and the other animals in the ocean. My dream is to inspire them to learn and make the world a better place.

Photo by Alex Bentley

Laura Barnes (O'Neill Sea Odyssey) and authors

From the Authors

Omar O. - age 11
"My favorite part is telling people about the garbage patch and saving the ocean."

Natalie R. - age 11
"My favorite part of writing the book is we get to make people realize that anyone could help clean the ocean."

Authors vote on their story ideas

Alex R. - age 12
"I like being able to tell people to clean up their trash."

Owen P. - age 11
"I think it's cool that you can write basically anything you want and have it in a book."

Marco C. - age 10
"I like teaching everyone about what they are doing with the trash."

Mariana H. - age 11
"I liked the writing and how we got to write independently and also writing with people."

Working out a part of the story

Analysia Y. - age 10
"My favorite part during the creation of the book was putting in and getting to hear great ideas."

Luella B. - age 11
"I like what the book is about and how we're educating people so the ocean will be safe and clean."

Nico V. - age 10
"I liked helping my friends so we could make a book."

Brian E. - age 12
"I like the book because we get to learn new things and I love the ocean."

Carlos A. - age 10
"I liked drawing the pictures."

Tyler D. - age 11
"I like being able to add anything you want to the story."

Explaining part of the story

Jose A. - age 11
"My favorite part of the book is when the monster wants the trash."

Jose A.

Claire R. - age 10
"I liked seeing my writing up on the walls."

Claire R.

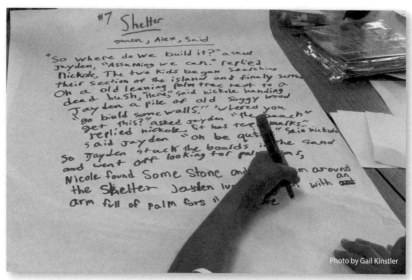

Writing the story

Angel G. - age 11
"I liked doing this because I was working with my team. I love to help the Earth be in a better place."

ANGE

Joshua S. - age 10
"I speak for the ocean and want to save the Earth."

Joshua.A

Kimberly M. - age 10

"I like writing with the group and what is going on in the story."

Cole L. - age 11

"I like the fact that we are teaching the world."

Describing a scene to the illustrator

Lizbeth A. - age 11

"The best part about the book was everything. It has action."

Kyla S. - age 10

"My favorite part about doing this is everything!"

Stephanie A. - age 10
"My favorite part of this book is that we get to tell everybody our ideas and that all our ideas are in this book! I like writing and looking at all the drawings that will be inside this book."

Stephanie A

Greta G. - age 10
"I really liked writing this book because it gives the world a kid's view of what grownups should do so there is less trash. It's just fun writing and giving ideas."

Greta G

Photo by Gail Kinstler

Acting out a scene

Jose H. - age 10
"I like that adults will be hearing our ideas."

Jose H

Aiden T. - age 10
"I like pretty much saving the ocean. I've always liked the ocean."

Aiden T.

Isai R. - age 11
"I think we can write about saving the ocean so other kids in the future have the same ocean."

Isai R

Said J. G. - age 11
"I liked seeing Joe's cartoons."

Said J

Photo by Alex Bentley

Sketching the authors' ideas

Xhunaxhi L. - age 10
"I guess I like all of the action and details. I like the drawings, all of them."

Xhunaxhi E. L. G.

Mariano L. - age 11
"This story is a really good story because other people wrote our ideas and the pictures are really nice."

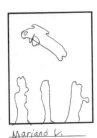

Mariano L.

What the authors want to say to the world

Researching story concepts

"Don't pollute!"

Nico V. - age 10

"I want to save the ocean."

Carlos A. - age 10

"I speak for the ocean and I won't let people throw trash in the ocean."

Brian E. - age 12

"Trashing the ocean is like trashing your home."

Tyler D. - age 11

"I would say to the world, 'Don't cut down those trees.'"

Angel G. - age 11

"Please stop littering and hurting the sea life. Try to clean up trash that you see lying around."

Claire R. - age 10

"We are writing this book so everyone will know to keep the world safe."

Natalie R. - age 10

"I speak for the ocean and marine life when I say, 'Stop polluting! Your trash is making it so others can't live!'"

Analysia Y. - age 10

"Don't pollute. Keep the world clean."

Mariana H. - age 11

"If I could say something to the world it would be, 'SAVE THE OCEAN!'"

Luella B. - age 11

Visualizing a swim scene

Trying to open a coconut

"I would say I speak for the animals because there is trash in the ocean."
Kimberly M. - age 10

"I want to tell the world to take care of everything because if you don't you will be seeing trash. Just trash!"
Lizbeth A. - age 11

"I want to tell the world about an actual and serious problem with the hope that we can make people stop littering. If there is no one who owns the ocean, it is everyone's job."
Cole L. - age 11

"Please help the ocean and save animals instead of not helping and killing animals, because my classmates and teacher care about the ocean!"
Kyla S. - age 10

"Help the world to be a better place to live."
Jose H. - age 10

"Please understand that we are killing our sea life and animal habitats. I am writing this book because I want to keep on living in a beautiful world, not a garbage world."
Stephanie A. - age 10

"Please be respectful to the Earth and keep it clean by not throwing trash away on the ground and please recycle."
Greta G. - age 10

Glossary

American Sign Language

The predominant sign language of deaf communities in the United States and English-speaking parts of Canada.

Atoll

A ring-shaped coral reef that encircles a lagoon.

Boat fender

In boating, a fender is a bumper used to absorb the energy of a boat when docked.

Crag

A steep rugged mass of rock projecting upward or outward

Gunnel

The top edge of the side of a boat

Gyre

An ocean gyre is a circular current formed by the Earth's wind patterns and the rotation of the planet.

Mast

A pole that holds a sail on sailing ships and boats.

Nudibranch

A group of soft-bodied, marine gastropod mollusks. They are noted for their extraordinary colors and striking forms.

Photo-degrade

To breakdown when exposed to sunlight. Plastic bags and bottles don't biodegrade. They only break down into tiny toxic little bits that pollute the soil and water. It takes around 1,000 years for plastic to break down in our landfills.

Rash-guard

A type of shirt made of spandex and nylon or polyester. It protects the wearer against rashes caused by abrasion or sunburn.

Stewardship

An ethic that embodies the responsible planning and management of resources.

Thermocline

A thin but distinct layer in a large body of fluid where the temperature is very different from the layers above or below.

Resources

http://www.ocean-sole.com/
http://5gyres.org/
http://education.nationalgeographic.com/education/encyclopedia/ocean-gyre/
http://www.gyrecleanup.org/
http://discovermagazine.com/2008/jul/10-the-worlds-largest-dump
http://www.theoceancleanup.com/
http://www.montereybayaquarium.org/
http://www.oneillseaodyssey.org/
http://rozaliaproject.org/

Good Search Terms

gyre

nurdles

plastic soup

Pacific Garbage Patch

ocean cleanup

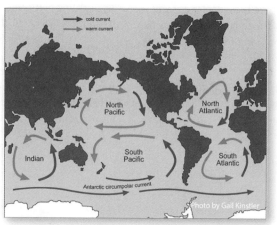

Gyres (from http://www.sciencelearn.org.nz/)

Don't Forget

Reduce

Reduce your use of non-reusable products.

Reuse

Find other uses for products instead of throwing them away.

Recycle

Recycle all you can.

Refuse

Don't get a plastic bag when you don't need one.

Find the hidden words.